For Edward

Hogs Back Books
The Stables
Down Place
Hogs Back
Guildford GU3 1DE
www.hogsbackbooks.com

First published in Great Britain in 2010 by Hogs Back Books Ltd

Designed by Louise Millar
Colour reproduction: Bright Arts (HK) Ltd
Printed in China

ISBN: 978-1-907432-00-2

British Library Cataloguing-in-Publication Data.
A catalogue record for this book is available from the British Library.

1 3 5 4 2

Hugh's Blue Day

Karen Hodgson and Ross Collins

Hogs Back Books

Hugh woke up in a grumpy mood.
He didn't like his clothes.
He didn't like his food.
He didn't like his cars.
He didn't like his planes.
He didn't like his trucks.
He didn't like his trains.

He didn't want to paint and
he didn't want to draw.

He lay down on the sofa
and did nothing at all.

"What's wrong?" asked Hugh's Mum.
"This isn't like you.
What's making you sad?
What's making you **blue**?"

"Don't know," said Hugh.
"Just don't want to play."
"Ok," said Mum,
"we'll have a **blue** day".

"A **blue** day?" asked Hugh.
"What do we do?"

"We have lots of fun
and make
EVERYTHING
blue!"

"First we put on **blue** trousers, **blue** vest and **blue** socks.

Then we find a shirt with **blue** stripes or **blue** spots."

"Won't work," said Hugh. "Just look at this shoe!
It's brown with black laces. There's no sign of **blue**."

"What about Wellies? They're more fun," said Mum.
"When splashing in puddles it's hard to feel glum."

"But first let's have breakfast.
What would you like best?

Six toast soldiers
and two dippy eggs?"

Hugh thought for a moment then let out a bellow,
"I can't eat eggs. They're white and yellow!"

"No, these eggs are different,
    today you're in luck.

They're not from a chicken;
they were laid by a duck."

When his teeth needed cleaning,
    Hugh faced the same plight.
The toothpaste was labelled

"But look very closely,
    there's a stripe running through!
        It's pink and it's white,
            and a tiny bit blue."

"It's time for school! Grab your bag and your hat!
In the cupboard downstairs there's a navy-**blue** mac."

"I can't go to school in our car. It's red!
Today's a blue day, that's what you said."

"Absolutely," said Mum. "No need to fuss.
We'll run up the lane and catch the **blue** bus."

On the top deck,
    the whole world whizzed by...

When Hugh got to school he was ready to play, with **blue** building bricks and **blue** modelling clay.

He ate **blue**-iced muffins and drank ice-**blue** milk shake,
but his **blue**-cheese sandwiches remained on the plate.

Yuk!

Home time came and Hugh left in a rush;
eager to ride again on the **blue** bus.

There were orange beans for supper
(from a greeny-**blue** can!).

And sponge for pudding
with **blue**berry jam.

Bath time was tricky –
the soap was pale green.

But the bath-foam bubbles were aquamarine.

Story time followed
    with Hugh's favourite books
Bluelocks and the Three Bears
    and **Blue** Riding Hood.

In his Dad's checked
pyjamas, Mum
tucked up her son,
"Our **blue** day is over.
Did you have fun?"

"Lots of fun Mummy,"
said Hugh with a grin.
"I love **blue** days.
Can we do it again?"

"**Blue** days are special –
once in a **blue** moon.
If you're a good boy,
one will come along soon."